D1499322

Jacob Goes to the Doctor
and
Sophie Visits the Dentist

By Sarah, Duchess of York

Illustrated by Ian Cunliffe

STERLING

New York / London

STERLING and the distinctive Sterling logo are registered trademarks of
Sterling Publishing Co., Inc.

Library of Congress Cataloging-in-Publication Data Available

Lot #:
2 4 6 8 10 9 7 5 3 1
10/10
Published by Sterling Publishing Co., Inc.
387 Park Avenue South, New York, NY 10016
Story and illustrations © 2007 by Startworks Ltd.
"Ten Helpful Hints" © 2009 by Startworks Ltd.
Distributed in Canada by Sterling Publishing
c/o Canadian Manda Group, 165 Dufferin Street
Toronto, Ontario, Canada M6K 3H6
Distributed in Australia by Capricorn Link (Australia) Pty. Ltd.
P.O. Box 704, Windsor, NSW 2756, Australia

Printed in China
All rights reserved.

Sterling ISBN 978-1-4027-7396-9

For information about custom editions, special sales, premium and
corporate purchases, please contact Sterling Special Sales
Department at 800-805-5489 or specialsales@sterlingpublishing.com.

R0433567881

All children face many new experiences as they grow up, and helping them to understand and deal with each is one of the most demanding and rewarding things we do as parents. Helping Hand Books are for both children and parents to read, perhaps together. Each simple story describes a childhood experience and shows some of the ways in which to make it a positive one. I do hope these books encourage children and parents to talk about these sometimes difficult issues. Talking together goes a long way to finding a solution.

Sarah,

Sarah, Duchess of York

Jacob couldn't understand it. He felt just fine. He counted all his fingers and toes and he still had ten of each! He wasn't sick, so why did he have to visit the doctor?

His mommy said that he had to go to the doctor for something called an injection. The injection would help make sure he did not get sick in the future.

"The doctors and nurses there will all be very nice," said his mommy.

"Are you coming with me?" Jacob asked nervously.

"Of course," said his mommy.

"And may I bring Sam and Rabbit and Moo-moo and Squiggles and—"

"You may bring only one of your toys," said his mommy. "But we will go and play in the park afterward."

When they arrived, the doctor's waiting room was busy.
A nice lady smiled at Jacob and asked him and his mommy
to wait for a few minutes. There were other people waiting,
too. Jacob and his mommy had fun looking at the tank full of
tropical fish.

Every few minutes a loudspeaker came on to call people to go see the doctor. Soon, the loudspeaker called Jacob's name.

"Will Jacob Edwards please go to room number eight?"

Jacob jumped to his feet. He had never been spoken to by a loudspeaker before! He squeezed his mommy's hand.

The nurse took Jacob and his mommy to a small room. His mommy helped him take off his shirt. Jacob held Rabbit tightly with one hand and his mommy with the other.

"Shall we give Rabbit an injection first?" asked the nurse, smiling.

"No!" said Jacob. "He's my favorite toy. He may not have ten fingers and toes but he's just fine, thank you."

"OK," said the nurse, "Why don't you and Mommy talk to Rabbit, then. I'll just wipe your arm with this cotton ball and . . . there! We're all done."

Jacob had felt a small sting in his arm. It felt kind of like a thorn prick, but it was all over in a second.

"Is that it?" asked Jacob.
The nurse nodded.

"Wow, that was easy!" said Jacob. Then he remembered about going to the park and the ice cream truck that was there.

"You can go now," said the nurse.

"You behaved so well today," said Jacob's mommy. "Would you like to get some ice cream?"

"Yippee!" said Jacob.

Rabbit smiled widely. He was excited for ice cream, too.

The next day in the playground, Jacob couldn't wait to tell his best friend Sophie all about his visit to the doctor.

But before he could say a word, Sophie—who liked to be first with a good story—announced, "I've been to the dentist!"

"That sounds scary," said Jacob.

"It was when we first got there," said Sophie. "But my mommy told me not to worry. She said all children have to go to the dentist to make sure their teeth are growing properly."

"One of mine fell out last week," said Jacob, eager to add to Sophie's story.

"The dentist was called Dr. Mason," said Sophie. "And he wore a white coat and white gloves. He was really nice."

"He asked me to sit in a big chair, and there was shiny equipment all around. Then he switched on a bright white light and asked me to open my mouth wide."

"Then the dentist asked me to say 'Aaah,'" said Sophie.

"That's funny. Why?" asked Jacob.

"So he could see my whole mouth," said Sophie.

"Aaaaaaaah!" Jacob practiced.

Sophie was a little annoyed that Jacob interrupted her. She continued her story.

"Then Dr. Mason took a look at my teeth with a little mirror and asked me to rinse out my mouth with a fizzy liquid," said Sophie. "It tasted yummy and minty. Then I opened wide again and said 'Ahhh' so Dr. Mason could finish looking at my teeth."

"Then he showed me how to brush my teeth properly. Dr. Mason said it is so easy for food to get stuck between my teeth. After the visit, he told my mommy he would like to see me again in six months."

"You have to go again?" Jacob asked.

"Yes," Sophie replied. "I'm not exactly looking forward to it, but I'm not worried about it either."

"Well, I think you were very brave," said Jacob. This made Sophie smile. "I went to see the doctor yesterday and it was just like that. Not too bad."

"That's good to know!" said Sophie. "My mommy is taking me to see the doctor next week."

"You can borrow Rabbit," said Jacob. "He made my visit so easy."

"Thanks," said Sophie. "I may need his help!"

TEN HELPFUL HINTS

WHEN TAKING YOUNG CHILDREN TO VISIT THE DOCTOR OR DENTIST

By Dr. Richard Woolfson, PhD

1. Don't tell your child about the visit at the last minute, but don't tell him too far in advance. The day before is long enough to allow you to answer your child's questions and have him get used to the idea. Answer his questions with positive and realistic replies at the level of detail suited to his age and understanding.

2. Point out all the benefits of going to visit the doctor or dentist. Explain to your child that the visit is to make her well again or to keep her healthy. Tell your child that the doctor or dentist has seen lots of other children before and is well-liked by them.

3. Tell your child what to expect when he is there. Give him some information about what the place looks like, who he will meet, and anything unfamiliar he might experience. This will help reduce the mystery, which will ease his anxiety.

4. Stay calm. Try to be as relaxed as possible. Your child can sense your anxiety and will react by getting anxious also.

5. Talk soothingly to your child. If you know she may become scared or tearful, soothe her even before she gets scared. Stroke her cheek gently and speak to her in a relaxed voice. Hearing your calming tone will reassure her sense of safety and well-being.

6. Tell your child that you are staying with him. Stay in your child's line of sight during the entire visit. You may even be able to hold his hand, depending on the nature of the examination.

7. Take along her favorite toy. Distraction is a simple technique, yet it frequently works. A young child's attention is easily drawn to something of interest even if she is upset.

8. Don't remove your child's clothes while waiting for the doctor or sit him in the dentist's chair until the last possible minute. For example, if you are asked to undress your two-year-old in preparation for the doctor's examination, wait until you know the doctor is ready. The longer he waits in an unfamiliar state, the more unsettled he might become.

9. Don't force your child's cooperation. Use persuasion and encouragement rather than compulsion. If she is not cooperating with the doctor's requests, use positive words, such as "You are such a brave girl" or "Please be good for the doctor." Try to avoid forcing her into the situation.

10. Should your child still refuse to cooperate, take some time out. Explain again the importance of this doctor or dentist visit. Allow him time to calm down, then try again. If absolutely necessary, make a second appointment and try again another day.

Dr. Richard Woolfson is a child psychologist, working with children and their families. He is also an author and has written several books on child development and family life, in addition to numerous articles for magazines and newspapers. Dr. Woolfson runs training workshops for parents and child care professionals and appears regularly on radio and television. He is a Fellow of the British Psychological Society.

Helping Hand Books

Look for these other helpful books to share with your child: